AF604493

Dear Grandpa

Jacinta Boyd

First published in Australia by Boolarong Press, 2022

ISBN: 978-1-922643-38-4

Boolarong Press
38/1631 Wynnum Road, Tingalpa, Qld, 4173, Australia
Supporting Australian Authors share their stories.

Text and illustrations © Jacinta Boyd 2022

All rights reserved. No part of this publication may be reproduced, stored in a retrieval system or transmitted in any form or by any means, electronic, mechanical, photocopying, recording or otherwise, without the prior permission of the publisher.

The author and publisher acknowledge the Traditional Custodians of Country on which this book was created, Wadawurrung Country. This book was published and printed on Quandamooka, Turrbal and Yuggera Country. We recognise First Nations Australians' rich, vibrant and precious culture and pay our respects to Elders past, present and emerging.

The illustrations in this book are hand painted with some digital retouching.
Typeset in Bookmania

This book is printed on Ecostar uncoated stock, 100% recycled and FSC certified.

A catalogue record for this book is available from the National Library of Australia

Graphic design and typesetting by Jacinta Boyd and Matthew Boyd
Proudly printed and bound in Australia by Boolarong Press

boolarongpress.com.au

For Dave and Ken and all the Grandpas, Pas and Poppys

And for my girls, Maeve and Hazel xx

Dear grandPa,

I haven't seen you in a while. You must be really busy.
I'm just wondering when you're coming to visit.
I've made a list of things we can do when you get here ...

When you come to visit, we can walk to the chocolate shop and buy giant lollipops and milky drops.

On clouds of fluffy white marshmallows
and cool, creamy ice-cream,
we can **dream.**

When you come to visit, we can sail across the rolling green seas in a shiny red boat.

Through waves that tumble and foam, we can **roam.**

When you come to visit, we can ride through the bush and look for enormous kangaroos and hiding black cats.

Where birds are made of rainbows
and foxes are furry and shy, we can **spy**.

When you come to visit, we can tiptoe over rambling rivers and slippery streams.

Swinging through the wild air,
with the wind in our hair, we can
explore, **without a care**.

When you come to visit, we can go swimming in the ocean among the shimmering fish and sunbaking seals.

In deep magical rock pools and the warm summer sun, we can have **fun.**

When you come to visit, we can dig in the garden where the beans grow like trees and tomatoes are the size of watermelons.

Where the wildflowers dance and
butterflies float and flutter,
we can **prance**.

When you come to visit, we can lie out under the stars, play games and tell silly jokes until the possums come out to play.

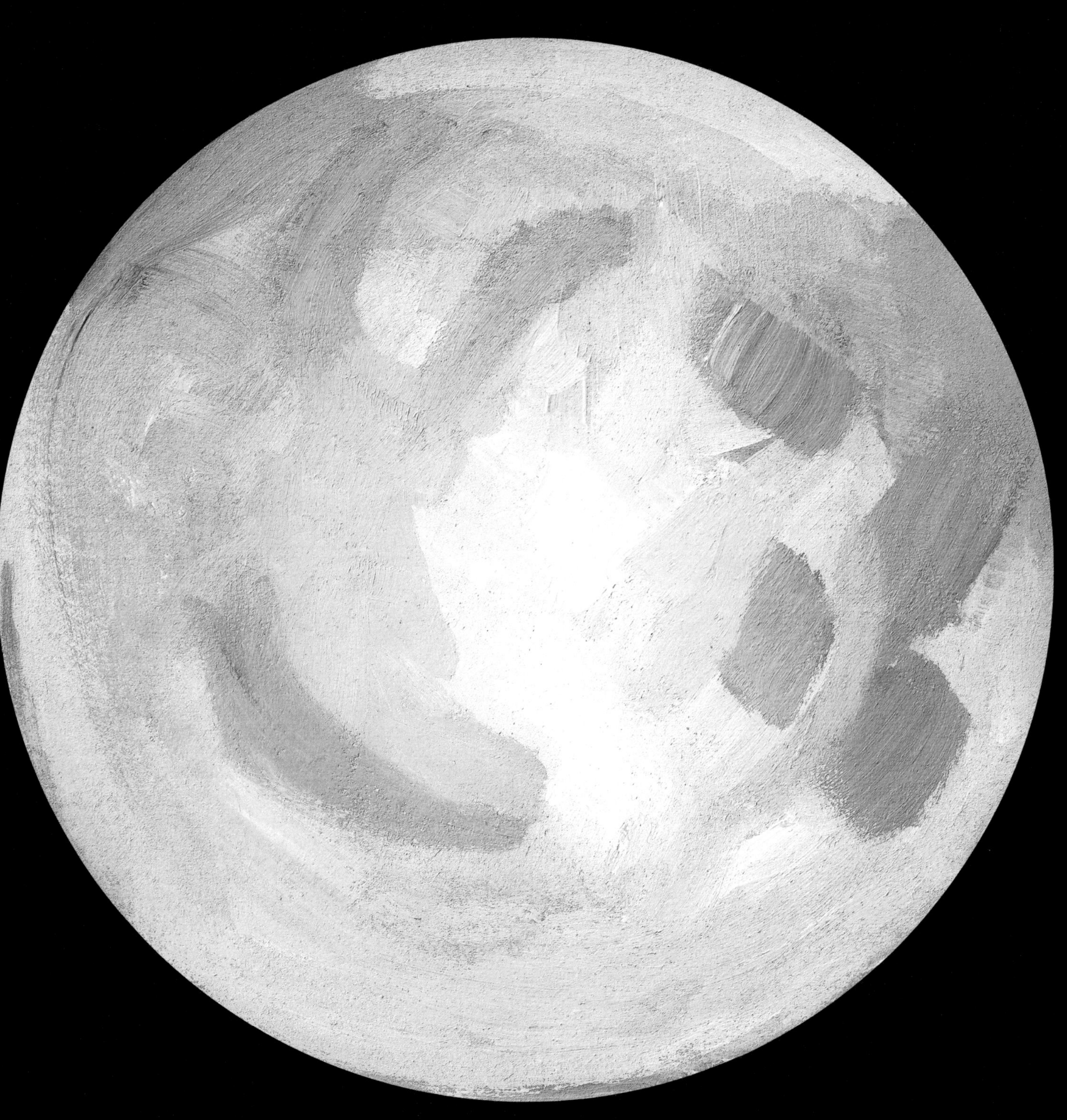

Under a dark, moonlit sky and a forest full of eyes,

we can **fly** ...

And when it's time for sleep,
you can tuck me in and tell me stories ...

... about a girl named Bea
and her amazing adventures with her Grandpa.

Dear Grandpa,
when are you coming to visit?

I miss you.

Love Bea xxx

Jacinta Boyd is an artist, author and illustrator. She is a qualified primary school teacher and graphic designer who lives with her husband and two daughters by the sea.

Her love of nature and finding joy in the simple things was instilled by her grandparents at a young age. *Dear Grandpa* is Jacinta's first published children's book.